Michael Bond
Paddington
at the
Tower

Illustrated by R. W. Alley

HarperCollins *Children's Books*

One of the nicest things about being a bear
and living with the Brown family was
that most days Paddington was able to share
his 'elevenses' with Mr Gruber.

So when he arrived at the bakers early one
morning to pick up their supply of buns and met
his best friend coming out he could hardly believe
his eyes. Such a thing had never happened before.

"I've closed my shop for the day," explained Mr
Gruber. "It's a long time since we had one of our
outings. Jonathan and Judy might like to come
along too. It will be their last chance before going
back to school."

Paddington needed no second bidding, and he rushed back home to number thirty-two Windsor Gardens as fast as his legs would carry him.

The Browns' housekeeper, Mrs Bird, was as excited as anyone and they ended up making so many sandwiches, Paddington had a job closing the lid of his suitcase.

"Bears always fall on their feet," she said.

In no time at all they were on their way.

"Where do you think we are going?" whispered Judy.

"You will find out soon enough," was all Mr Gruber would say. "Wait and see."

It was a long journey right across London but suddenly they turned a corner and came to a stop.

"It's the Tower of London!" chorused Jonathan and Judy excitedly.

While Mr Gruber went to collect the tickets to go in, Paddington took a closer look.

"I've never seen anything quite so big!" he said to the man at the security check.

"And I've never seen so many marmalade sandwiches," said the man, looking into his suitcase. He was about to feel underneath them, but he thought better of it.

"That man didn't find my secret compartment,"
called Paddington, as he hurried after the others.

"Ssh!" hissed Judy. She pointed to a man in a
dark blue uniform standing nearby. "That's a
Yeoman of the Guard. They're called 'Beefeaters'
and they keep a look-out for anything suspicious."

"I hope you didn't hear what I said," exclaimed Paddington, addressing the Beefeater.

"No," said the man. "I can't say as I did."

Paddington was most relieved. He raised his hat politely and as he did so something fell out and landed on the man's highly-polished boots.

"It's a marmalade sandwich," he explained. "I couldn't get them all in my suitcase. You can have it if you like. I expect it will make a change from beef."

"A MARMALADE SANDWICH!" repeated the Yeoman. He gazed down at his boots, but by the time he looked up Paddington had already disappeared.

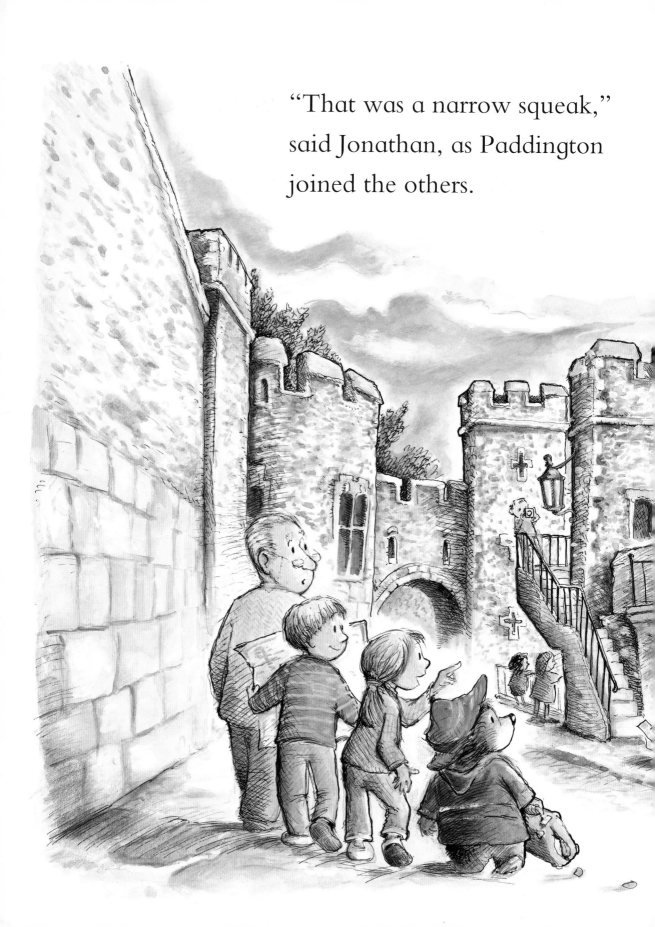

"That was a narrow squeak," said Jonathan, as Paddington joined the others.

Judy pointed towards a large black bird.

"If you ask me, that raven has got his eye on your sandwich too."

"Perhaps," suggested Mr Gruber hastily, "we should visit the Crown Jewels."

Paddington thought it was a very good idea until
he saw the queue going in. "I shall never see over
all those heads," he said.

"Don't worry, Mr Brown," called Mr Gruber.
"Follow me."

And he led them on to a moving walkway where they had a good view of all the exhibits as they glided past them.

Paddington was most impressed. "They've thought of everything at the Tower," he said.

"I've never been on a moving floor before," said Paddington as they reached the end of it. "I wouldn't mind going round again."

"I don't think we would be very popular if we did that," said Mr Gruber. He pointed to another display case instead. "That's the Imperial Crown of India. It has over six thousand diamonds, but the Queen never uses it."

"I'm not surprised," said Paddington. "There's nowhere to keep her sandwiches. She ought to have a hat like mine."

The next exhibit was a huge golden bowl the size of a small bathtub.

"That was for holding wine," explained Mr Gruber. "I don't suppose you had anything like that in Darkest Peru."

"We had a big bath in the Home for Retired Bears," said Paddington. "Except it wasn't made of gold and there was a big queue for it on Friday nights."

He licked his lips. "They made cocoa in it the rest of the week."

Mr Gruber took the hint. "I think it's time for our elevenses," he said.

"That's funny," said Jonathan, as they made
their way outside. "There are three ravens now."

Paddington eyed the birds uneasily as they
waddled towards him.

"Look!" said Judy, pointing straight ahead.
"The Ravens tea house! We must be near where
they live."

"I wonder if they have a Bears tea house?"
said Paddington.

"I doubt it," said Mr Gruber. "In the old days
there were lots of wild animals at the Tower...
lions and tigers and such-like... but there aren't
any more. They all went to Regent's Park Zoo."

"I think I'll just have a small lemonade if I
may, Mr Gruber," said Paddington. "They might
have left a lion behind by mistake."

By now two more
ravens had joined the others,
making five in all. "They
must be after something," said
Mr Gruber. "I wonder what
it can possibly be?"

While he was talking a sixth
raven landed.

"I think he's after your suitcase, Paddington,"
warned Jonathan.

Paddington gave the bird a hard stare, and
he was about to shoo it away when he heard
a familiar voice.

"There he is," said the Beefeater, addressing
a grey-haired gentleman. "I'd know him
anywhere. Blue duffle coat, red hat, suitcase..."

"Oh, dear," said Judy, as the man came
towards their table. "What now?"

Paddington felt his knees turn to jelly.

But the grey-haired gentleman was all smiles.
"I didn't know ravens like marmalade," he said.
"The Tower of London is famous for its ravens,
but there is a legend which says if ever they fly
away it will fall down, so anything which stops
that happening is most welcome. I have been
instructed to present you with a special ticket that
will enable you to visit us from
now on, whenever you
like, free of charge."
"You will need proof
of identity," warned
the Beefeater.

"Otherwise you won't be allowed in."

"I think his suitcase will do the trick," said the man. "There can't be many people who carry a case full of marmalade sandwiches around with them."

"I'm sure Mrs Bird can arrange that," said Mr Gruber. "What do you think, Mr Brown?"

"I think," said Paddington, "I had better start work straight away. It has been such a lovely day out, I must make sure the Tower doesn't fall down before we come again."

"Caw! Caw!" said the ravens. "Caw! Caw!"

Look out for more fantastic books about Paddington!

Paddington
at the Palace

Michael
Bond

*Illustrated by
R. W. Alley*

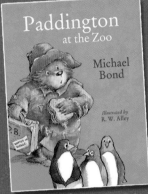

Paddington
at the Zoo

Michael
Bond

*Illustrated by
R. W. Alley*

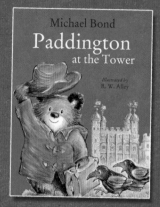

Michael Bond
Paddington
at the Tower

*Illustrated by
R. W. Alley*

Michael Bond
Paddington
the Artist

*Illustrated by
R. W. Alley*

Paddington
Michael Bond

*Illustrated by
R. W. Alley*

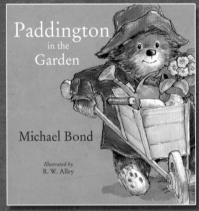

Paddington
in the
Garden

Michael Bond

*Illustrated by
R. W. Alley*

Michael Bond

Paddington
and the
Grand Tour

Illustrated by R. W. Alley

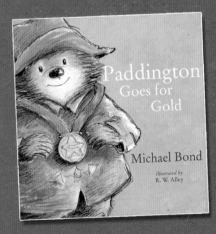

Paddington
Goes for
Gold

Michael Bond

*Illustrated by
R. W. Alley*

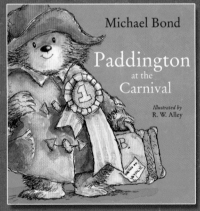

Michael Bond

Paddington
at the
Carnival

*Illustrated by
R. W. Alley*

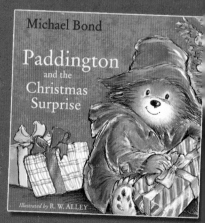

Michael Bond

Paddington
and the
Christmas
Surprise

Illustrated by R. W. ALLEY

HarperCollins *Children's Books*